D0185701

COLUMBA AND THE MONSTROUS WURRRM

TWELVE HIGHLAND TALES

By
Elizabeth Sutherland

Illustrated by
Lizzie McDougall

First published 2012

by

Moving Arts
Conon Brae, Ross-shire
IV7 8AG
lizzie.mcdougall@gmail.com

Text Copyright: Elizabeth Sutherland
Illustrations Copyright: Lizzie McDougall

The moral rights of the authors has been asserted
All rights reserved

ISBN 978-1-905787-58-6

Printed by
'For The Right Reasons'
60 Grant Street
Inverness
IV3 8BS
fortherightreasons@rocketmail.com

COLUMBA AND THE MONSTROUS WURRRM

TWELVE HIGHLAND TALES

COLUMBA AND THE MONSTROUS WURRRM

TWELVE HIGHLAND TALES

These little stories have been told and re-told over the years, some as long ago as the seventh century when St Adomnan, who called the Loch Ness Monster, a 'monstrous wurm', wrote his hagiography of St Columba. Others have been re-told by the folklorists Otta Swire, Hugh Miller, Fiona Macleod (William Sharp) and Alexander Mackenzie, who, like all good story-tellers, have interpreted them in their own inimitable way. Intended to be enjoyed by all age groups, these little tales reveal what our forebears thought, believed and feared. Mankind has never existed without stories and we are no different today. These ancient tales deserve to be told yet again to a new generation and in a new way. In this short collection, they are given new life by the illustrations of artist, Lizzie McDougall and the words of writer, Elizabeth Sutherland.

DEIRDRE OF THE STARRY EYES

Deirdre was the most beautiful maiden in all Ulster. Her lips were as red as the raven's blood, her hair as black as the raven's wing and her eyes brighter than all the stars in heaven.

King Conachar fell in love with her at first sight, but when his druid, Cathbad, saw her, he tore his hair. 'You cannot marry this woman,' he told the king, 'for it has been foreseen, she will be the downfall of Ireland.'

'If I cannot marry her then no one shall,' the king declared savagely and ordered that she be shut up in a lonely tower where none would find her.

Now the king had three young cousins called Naois, Aillean and Ardan who had heard of Deirdre's beauty. Eager to see her, they paid the king a visit. 'Where is Deirdre of the Starry Eyes?' they asked him 'That is not for you to know,' the king replied sternly and offered them a day's hunting in the forest.

Deirdre's old nurse knew where she was hidden, and, because she was angry with the king for hiding the maiden away, she came to the three brothers by night and told them where to find her.

Next morning, instead of hunting, the three young men and their followers took off by themselves. They soon found the tower and Deirdre within, more beautiful than a dream. They all fell in love with her starry eyes but she fell in love with Naois. 'Take me away from here,' she begged him, so Naois promised to help her, and his brothers swore to help him.

Secretly they made their plans and when the time was right they fled by night on horseback to the sea and from thence across the water into the land of mountains that lay beyond. Day after day they travelled east until they came to the fertile banks of a great stretch of water where the salmon leapt and the stags roared. 'This is the place,' they declared to each other. 'Here we will remain.'

The water they called Loch Naois, and the house they built was Dun Dearduil, the Fortress of Deirdre. Here they were happy, but not for long.

King Conachar, when he heard of the trick his cousins had played on him, reddened with rage and plotted how he might take his revenge. Fergus mac Ro, who had a smooth tongue and a beguiling manner, was sent to Loch Naois with offers of peace and forgiveness if only the king's three cousins would return to Ulster.

Deirdre and Naois and his brothers listened to all that he had to say, but Deirdre warned them, 'The promises of the king sound fair, but, I tell you, his heart is false.' The brothers, however, missed Ireland, so they accepted the king's word and returned. The moment they set foot in Ulster they were seized and murdered by the cruel king. Their bodies were cast into a single grave by a running stream.

In sorrow Deirdre looked down upon the open grave and cried, 'Let Naois my true love move to one side and let Aillean press closer to Ardan. If the dead could only hear me, they would make room for me.' When the brothers heard her they moved and she lay down by her husband's side and died of grief.

King Conachar was so angry that he had her body removed to the opposite bank of the stream, but even in death he could not separate them. Out of each grave there grew tree, a beech and an oak, whose branches leaned ever closer together across the water, until, in no time at all, they grew into one great tree.

Loch Naois became known as Loch Ness and you can still visit the remains of Dun Dearduil.

THE MONSTROUS WURRM OF LOCH NESS

Everyone knows the story of how Columba on his visit to King Brude told the monstrous wurrm that lived in the River Ness to behave itself and how it slunk back into the river and sulked. Perhaps you don't know what happened next?

The time came for Columba to leave Craig Phadraig, the fortress of King Brude. The king had given him many generous parting gifts, including the island of Iona, so the day finally arrived for him to leave Inverness. After a farewell feast, he and his two friends set out in their coracle to row west up the river and sail down the whole length of Loch Ness. They had barely reached the beginning of the loch when a great storm of wind and rain and hail and thunder arose. Columba's companions said it was the work of the druid Briochan but he only laughed. 'No,' he said 'Briochan's magic cannot touch us now. Be of good courage, my friends. God will protect us.'

But it was not God whose massive head reared up out of the water and shook its wet snaky locks at them. No indeed! It was the monstrous wurrm and it was swimming towards them on the crest of a great wave as fast as the wind itself. Columba's companions were afraid. 'It has come to have its revenge,' they warned Columba. 'Ochone and ochone it will swallow us whole.'

But Columba was not afraid. He rose to his feet in the teeth of the wind while the hail battered his face and the rain soaked his clothing. With one hand he held on to the mast while with the other he raised his cross. 'Peace be with you, my friend!' he called out in that great voice of his, as loud as the wind itself. 'A blessing upon your head.'

The monster reared its long wurrmy neck up over the little boat and roared while the two companions cowered and covered their heads with their hands. 'Ochone and ochone,' they lamented again and again. Then with a mighty roar that sounded like thunder it lowered its great head and shook it from side to side as if searching for something.

Suddenly its long neck darted forwards and its wide mouth seized - not Columba nor his friends - but the coiled rope that was used to tether the boat to the pier. Then it turned with the end of the rope clutched tightly in its great mouth and pulled the

little boat safely through the teeth of the gale all the way down the long length of Loch Ness.

It was the most wonderful ride, up and down on the waves with the spray splashing their faces. Columba and his friends would remember it for the rest of their lives.

Very gently it dropped the rope back on to the boat and bowed its great head. Columba raised his cross staff again. 'The blessing of the great Father be upon you. For this deed that you have done today, God has granted you the freedom of Loch Ness for ever.'

With a great roar of joy the monstrous wurrm turned, dived into the deep water and was seen by men no more. Sometimes, however, its coils can still be glimpsed trawling the loch as if looking for the saint who once blessed it.

THE HEALING STONE OF *BANATH*

The Pictish druid, Briochan, did not like the Irish druid, Columba, because he had new ways and new ideas and a new magic that he called Christianity.

His song had flung open the locked gates of Craig Phadraig. His command had tamed the monstrous wurrrm that haunted Loch Ness, and, with his wooden cross, he had calmed the raging storm that Briochan himself had raised to drown him in his coracle. His gentle eyes had endeared him to womenfolk while his craic made King Brude laugh. Briochan feared for his job.

But there was someone Columba could not have for all his singing, his craic and his magic, for she belonged to Briochan and Briochan would never part with her. She had grown up in his household, and, although she was as a daughter to him, she was his slave.

'It is not fitting that you should keep her as a slave for she is from Derry and she is a Christian,' Columba told him.

'You shall never have her,' Briochan declared, 'unless it be over my dead body.'

That was an unfortunate thing to say to a powerful druid. Briochan knew it, but the words could not be unsaid.

That very day he was stricken with a seizure. He lay on his bed, his eyes staring, his mouth open, his slave in attendance. King Brude himself came to see him. He shook his head for he knew his old druid was close to death. 'There is only one who can help him now,' the king declared.

Messengers were sent to search for Columba. 'He is alone on the shore,' they were told. 'He is at prayer.'

Sure enough they found him at *Ban Ath*, the White Ford on the River Ness, so called for the wealth of white pebbles that were scattered on the shore. They told him of Briochan's seizure. 'Unless you can heal him, he will surely die,' they explained.

Bending down, he picked up one of the pebbles, a perfect little moon of a stone, held it up to the sunlight and blessed it. Then he gave it to one of the messengers. 'Take this to your druid. He knows what he must do.'

The king himself took it into Briochan's chamber. Himself he held it before the old man's staring eyes, but he did not stir.

‘Give it to me,’ whispered the slave girl from Derry. She held it to his brow and sure enough the old man blinked his eyes and his strength returned. They told him what had happened and how he had been saved from death by the magic stone from Columba. He listened carefully to all they told him and then he beckoned to his slave.

Go now,’ he told her. ‘Go to the Christian druid. You are free.’ Those who were closest to him saw tears in his eyes.

Columba was still by the shore. He sat on the grassy bank and looked up when the girl approached. ‘I am free,’ she told him.

‘I am glad to hear it.’

‘But,’ she cried, falling to her knees before him in tears, ‘I am not free. I love my master as my father. There is no freedom for me away from him.’

Columba rose and drew her to her feet. ‘Then return to him, daughter of Derry. Perfect freedom lies in the service of others.’

So she did and Columba and Briochan were reconciled. As for King Brude, he placed the healing stone carefully in his treasure chest against his own dying. Strangely enough, when that time came, it had disappeared. Some say it found its own way back to *Ban Ath*, the White Ford.

THE GUARDIAN OF THE WELL

Believe it or not, there was a time when there was no water in Loch Ness.

Who said so? Daly said so and Daly knows everything.

Instead of the loch, a deep dark valley stretched between the great mountains and at the very centre of it, there was a well.

Who said so? Daly said so, and Daly knows, for he was once the Druid of those parts and Daly knew everything. When the young girls asked when was it time to wash their faces in the May dew, he rang his bell at dawn on Beltane morning to awaken them. When the women asked when was it time to clean out their hearths, Daly rang his bell on the morning of Imbolc. When the crofters asked was it time to prepare for Harvest, he rang his bell all day at Lammas. When the young lads asked was it time to go guising, he would ring his bell at dusk to announce that now it was Samhain.

Daly was also Guardian of the Well and Daly had rules. All were welcome to take the water, which was sweeter than June sunlight and sparklier than December frost, so long as each put back the big round stone that covered the well. Even if there was a tail of women stretching the length of the glen waiting for water, each one had to replace the cap before the next in line filled her bucket. Even if it was only a drink you were wanting. That was the rule.

Daly the Druid sat beside the well under an ancient oak tree whose branches stretched up into the clouds. It was difficult to tell where the tree started and Daly began because they were both so gnarled and wrinkled and old. Sometimes the women thought it was the tree itself that growled at them, 'Put back the stone, woman, or it will be the worse for us all.'

One hot Lammastide noon, a woman called Mairi who lived in a croft in the glen came for water. Mostly the women came at dawn or in the cool of dusk to fill their buckets, but Mairi's new baby, who had cried all night, had finally fallen asleep. He looked so peaceful curled up in his cradle that she picked up her bucket and whispered to him, 'I'll be back before you know it, little lamb.'

Everyone, it seemed, was asleep including Daly the Druid under the towering branches of his aged oak tree. Bees buzzed and lots of little beasties hummed their summer songs. No one was about.

Quietly, carefully, Mairi lifted off the stone cap and lowered her bucket. The cool dark water winked enticingly up at her from the bottom of the well.

She pulled up her brimming bucket and put it down to replace the stone cap. It was in her hands when she heard her baby cry. 'Wah, wah, wah,' it wailed. Mairi dropped the stone, grabbed her pail and ran.

The water saw its chance. Quietly it rose up to the top of the parapet, Quickly it spilled over in a great cool sheet. Daly awoke. He grabbed his bell and rang it loudly. 'Tha loch nis ann! Tha loch nis ann!' he shouted. Men came running from their fields searching for the stone cap to cover the well but no one could find it. The crofters grabbed their children and fled into the hills. The water lifted Daly high into the top branches of his tree and then it stopped and became Loch Ness.

I'm told Daly is still there and if you listen very hard on a windy night you will hear him say, 'Tha loch nis ann! Tha loch nis ann!'

THE WIZARD OF KILLIN

Once upon a time there was a wizard who lived in a barren croft in the far north. After many years of experiment, he invented a spell whereby he could steal the fertility of the nine richest glens in Scotland to enrich his own croft where the ground was stony, the earth acid, and his cattle starved. So off he set and, after a year and a day, he came to the glen of Killin on the River Fechlin which snuggles between the Monadliath Mountains high above Loch Ness.

Bound to his back with withy straps, he carried the substance of eight fertile glens and he was weary. One glen only remained and then he could return to his croft in the north and live in comfort for the rest of his life watching his corn flourish and his cattle grow fat.

He did not know, however, that there lived in Killin another wizard whose magic eye told him what was happening. From his croft he watched the weary magician bowed under the weight of the withy bundles on the path beside the river, so down he sped to meet him.

'Good day to you, friend,' he declared cheerfully. 'What a load you are carrying. Let me help you with it.'

‘I thank you, friend, but I can manage well enough,’ he answered without stopping.

‘I insist on helping you, my friend,’ said the local wizard standing in front of him and blocking his path.

‘No indeed, though you are kind to offer.’ The wizard from the north was not in the least afraid because he had protected his bundles with a spell. No one could take them from him. Others had tried and had been blown away for their trouble.

But the wizard of Killin knew about magic. He knew that no spell can be stronger than the power of iron. As the stranger passed him on the road, he took out his iron knife and snip, snap snip, he cut the withy straps. Out tumbled the rich substance of the eight glens into the ninth.

From that day to this, Glen Killin has flowed with milk and honey. So it is said.

TWO TALES OF STRATHERRICK

THE CASK'S LEAP

After the terrible Battle of Culloden in 1746, James Fraser the laird of Foyers escaped with his life. Though the Redcoats were after him and there was a price on his head, the clans hid him and fed him for seven long years in a cave above the Falls.

Nicknamed Dun Bonnet, the laird could see everyone and everything that was going on around him. One day while he was watching the young girl who was bringing him his food for the day, he saw that she was being followed by a Redcoat. So he waited until he was within range, shot him and threw his body down the falls.

On another occasion while a young boy was bringing him a small cask of beer, he was stopped by a troop of Redcoats who immediately guessed where he was going.

'Now we have him,' the officer crowed.' Lead us to your master, boy. I order you.'

But the brave lad shook his head. Though they taunted him, threatened his with their swords, and swore at him he held his tongue. Finally the officer lost patience, lifted his hand and gave the boy a resounding smack. He dropped the cask. Immediately it rolled away and tumbled down into the depth of the Falls. To this day that place is known as the Cask's Leap.

As for Dun Bonnet he survived to be one of the more fortunate lairds to hold on to his land in Stratherrrick.

THE LOST HORSE

Three clans lived in Stratherrick - the Grants, the Cummins and the Frasers - and fiercesome were the feuds and fights between them. One night a favourite dun-coloured horse was lifted from a croft belonging to one of the Grants who had fallen on hard times. Great were the recriminations and oaths and searchings but no trace of it was found, no thief exposed.

The following Christmas during a great storm the crofter's wife was disturbed by a familiar sound. She shook her husband awake. 'Listen, husband,' she whispered. 'If he be alive and above the earth, that is the neigh of our own lost horse.'

'Woman, you are right!' he cried, leaping from the bed. When he opened the door, there stood the beautiful horse, head bowed against the storm. So

glad was he to see it that he welcomed it into his own fireside. What a Christmas present that was, but there was more. Bound to its back were two barrels of whisky worth a fortune and tied to its tail was a sturdy little pony. God was good indeed.

So what had happened? No one knew. No one came forward to claim the whisky or the pony. It was thought that the horse had been stolen in the first place by the distillers of Ferintosh in the Black Isle and that it had escaped in the storm to find its own way back to its true home. Who cared anyway? That was a memorable Christmas in Stratherrick.

BLESS THE FAIRIES!

Everyone knows that fairies were the first creatures ever to inhabit the Fairy Glen in the village of Rosemarkie in the Black Isle.

There they lived on the whole peaceably with their human neighbours who had learned from experience that it was best to keep in with them. In exchange for a copper penny hammered into a tree, or a scrap of lace left beside the third waterfall, they might clear a field of weeds or stack your peats neatly behind your house. Falling out with the fairies was not a good idea. They might steal your baby from its cradle or bewitch your man into a drunken madness. So it was said. So it was believed.

Only one man could control the fairies. He was the great wizard, Michael Scot. He could get them to do anything he wanted, build a bothy, or a croft, a castle or even a cathedral. Two cathedrals in fact, one in Elgin and one in Fortrose. The trouble was that the fairies of Rosemarkie never got their tasks quite right. Their bothies had leaking roofs, their crofts had crooked chimneys, their castles had missing stairways. As for the cathedrals, Fortrose Kirk, which was big and grand, was built in Elgin and Elgin Kirk, which was smaller and not so grand, was built in Fortrose. The Bishop of Ross was not best pleased, as you can imagine.

After the cathedrals were finished, the fairies took a craze for building. No sooner had they completed one task than they craved to do another. 'Give us more work,' they clamoured in their dozens at Michael's door and in Michael's head. 'More work! More work! More work!''

Michael was at his wits end to think up tasks for them.

One day while he was sitting outside his croft enjoying the sunset over the Moray Firth, they started their buzzing like midges all round him. In desperation, he told them to build a road across the Moray Firth. That would surely get them out of his head for a while.

Off they flew with their wee spades, their axes and hammers, their fairy ponies and little basket carts, delighted with the task. Starting at Rosemarkie, they piled the pink sand and the big rocks, the little shells and the gravel into a great road that began to stretch across the water towards Ardersier.

What a grand job they were making of it! The weavers in Rosemarkie were delighted. 'This way we can trade our linen with the people of Moray and

we can get rich.' The shoemakers in Fortrose, too, were pleased. 'This way we can make shoes for the people of Nairn and get rich' Everyone was pleased. As for Michael Scot, he was delighted to have the fairies out of his head for a while at least.

Oh, but you have to be so careful with fairies! Mostly the humans left them well alone to get on with their work.

One day a kindly old man from Rosemarkie, determined to thank them, set off along the new road, nearly a mile of it finished and sticking right out into the Firth to where the dolphins play. There they were, all busy-busy, digging and hammering and loading their little creels with gravel and sand. Full of admiration, he watched them for a while from behind a whin bush. Then he stepped out and shouted out in a loud voice. 'This is a good work you are doing. God bless ye, little men!'

In a trice they vanished, every single one of them. They changed into a swarm of midges and disappeared from Rosemarkie forever. The old man had forgotten that fairies vanish at the very hint of God's name. As for Michael Scot, he was never bothered by them again.

THE LITTLE MEN OF EATHIE GLEN

So where did they go to, the little men with their spades and their hammers and their wee ponies? I'll tell you. They went to the Eathie Glen near Cromarty which is a wild steep place where roses and sloe thorns snag the deer, and old trees fall down upon new trees and the water rushes through a steep rocky ravine. Donald-the-shop will tell you for he heard them one moonlit night as he travelled from business in Fortrose, stopping by the taverns in Rosemarkie, back to his shop in Cromarty.

He had just reached the ford where the Eathie burn flattens itself out for travellers when he heard music. So beautiful it was, that he stood still just to listen and what he heard was this; a thousand little voices singing his name. 'Hi, Donnie Calder! Ho, Donnie Calder! Are you coming Donnie Calder? You are welcome, Donnie Calder!'

'I'm coming,' he cried and splashed through the ford. But when he reached the other bank the music had ceased. There was nothing but the trickle of the water and no-one to be seen and nowhere for singers to hide.

He was about to continue on his journey when he heard the song again, sweeter than ever. This time it was coming from the side of the burn he had just left.

'Are ye coming Donnie Calder? We're awaiting, Donnie Calder. Make haste, Donnie Calder!' the voices sang beguilingly.

'I'm coming,' he cried, so back he splashed across the burn only to hear the voices on the far side as before. Back and forth he went all night long, looking for the musicians and their welcome, until, at length, when the sun rose, the voices ceased.

Finally he limped home, worn and weary, but he never found the musicians.

He knew he had heard the fairies.

Only two human beings that I know of have ever seen them.

A young lad and his sister were herding cattle one night by the banks of the Eathie burn, when, in the moonlight, they saw a strange sight. A column of little men, each of them about a meter tall, were winding their way down the steep glen on the opposite bank of the burn. Dressed in grey with bright red caps on their shaggy heads, they were leading little ponies drawing basket-woven carts

laden with bundles and sacks. Their heads were bowed and their backs were bent.

The boy called out bravely, ‘Who are ye, little men?’

The last in the column turned his head. ‘Farewell, son of Adam,’ he called out sadly. ‘We are the last of our race. The likes of us will never be seen again among the children of men.’

They never said where they were going, they never said why, but they spoke the truth. They have never been seen since.

THE SHEPHERD OF KINTAIL

Iain the Shepherd lived in a bothy by himself high up in the mountains of Kintail. Every day, he put on his shepherd's plaid and his black cap which his mother had knitted for him and he went out into the hills to watch over his sheep.

One stormy night after he had seen that his sheep were safe and sound, he returned to his bothy. He hung up his black cap on a nail by the window, lit himself a bright cheerful fire and threw himself down on his heather bed, glad to rest after a busy day on the hill. Half-asleep, he saw the latch on his door open and in stalked a black cat. It sat down by the fire and held up its paws to the warmth. After a short while another cat walked in, and another and another until there were twenty cats sitting in front of his fire, holding out their paws and warming themselves.

The first one got up, stalked over to the window, and, picking up the shepherd's black cap, put it on his head and cried, 'Hurrah for London!' Immediately it vanished leaving nothing but the cap behind. One by one, all the other cats did the same until only the cap was left.

The shepherd, being curious, rose from his bed, went over to the window, put on his cap, held on to it tight and cried, 'Hurrah for London!' In a trice he found himself, still wearing his cap, in a cellar in London with the cats and they were all drinking wine.

Next morning he awoke with a very sore head. The cats had all disappeared. He was alone in the cellar surrounded by a sea of empty bottles. When the owner of the wine cellar arrived and saw that his store of wine had been drunk, he had him arrested and brought to trial. The judge pronounced him guilty of theft and sentenced him to be hanged to death within the week.

As he stood on the gallows, he pleaded to be allowed to wear the cap he had been wearing in the cellar. 'It was a present from my mother. She knitted it herself,' he told the executioner, who, being a sentimental sort of fellow, ordered the cap to be brought. When it came, the noose was already round his neck.

Clapping the hat on his head he cried, 'Hurrah for Kintail!' He was in such a state, however, that he forgot to hold on to his cap. Immediately he disappeared. At the same time, he turned up in his own bothy which was full of his friends and

relations. They were about to send out a search party for he had been missing all week.

They were glad to welcome him back, safe and sound, but mightily surprised to see a rope noose around his neck. As for the black knitted cap, he never saw it again, which was perhaps just as well.

BRIDE AND THE SNOWDROPS

Cathal, the ancient arch-druid of all Ireland, came to Dugald Dubh leading a small child by the hand. 'Find yourself a wife, Dugald. Together you shall care for this child who is one of the Immortals. Through her, a prophecy is to be fulfilled: '*My garment shall be laid on the Lord of the World, the King of the Elements Himself.*'

So Dugald married the woman of his heart and together they took the child to Iona which was then called the sacred Isle of the Druids. There on the slope of Dun I, he lived as a poor herdsman and watched the golden-haired Bride grow in beauty and harmony with the earth and the cattle she birthed and loved.

Not far from the summit of Dun I, there is a pool called to this day the Fountain of Youth. Here she would go to watch the great sun-god rise, fill her pitcher and lead her cattle to drink the sweet cool water. There was no place on all the island that she loved so well.

One morning, just before sunrise, as she approached the pool with her pitcher on her arm and the cattle at her heels, she heard her name.

'Bride, Exalted One, your time has come.'

Cathal, the ancient arch-druid of all Ireland, stood before her dressed in a white robe, his long flowing white hair encircled with oak leaves.

'How so?' she asked shyly.

'Look you in the water and follow your destiny.'

So Bride knelt down on the grassy bank and gazed into the clear water of the pool. There she saw a woman who was not like herself, but dark and beautiful beyond belief. The woman reached out her arms to Bride and spoke two words, 'Help me.'

'I will,' Bride cried. 'Indeed, I will!'

At that moment her cattle reached the pool, and, when they drank, the image broke up and vanished. Cathal too had gone.

'How am I to find you?' Bride cried out.

Even as she spoke, two rowan trees on the far side of the pool reached out their branches towards each other. They intertwined to make a deep green arch. So, picking up her pitcher of water, she followed it through darkness and emerged into light…and heat and sand and a different sea. She knew she was in a strange land.

A great sea bird flew past her and she cried out, 'Tell me, sea bird, which way should I go?'

The sea bird answered, 'This way, O Bride, Bride, Bride, Bri-i-ide.'

So she followed him till she could see him no more. From that day on the oyster catcher has been called the Gille-Brighde, the Servant of Bride.

Bewildered she stood and looked around her. A bee fluttered and buzzed about her head. ‘Tell me, little bee, which way should I go?’

‘Follow me, follow me,’ the bee buzzed about her head. So she followed it until it vanished inside a snowdrop.

‘Which way now?’ she asked, for she was growing tired and the pitcher of water was heavy on her hip.

There before her lay a path of little white flowers, which grew and lengthened as she followed. Still they sprang up ahead of her until they stopped outside the mouth of a cave.

It was there that she found the beautiful lady she had seen in the Fountain of Youth, and, indeed and indeed, the lady was in need of her help.

When the child was born, Bride wrapped him in her own mantle and laid him in his mother’s arms. Thus was the ancient prophecy fulfilled when she laid her garment on the King of the Elements. For six weeks she tended them both until Candlemas when the time came for her to return to Iona.

As before, the Servant of Bride was waiting to lead her to the shore, and, when he had gone, the little golden bee was ready to take her to the green arch of the quicken trees. Snowdrops sprang up joyfully at her feet and spread like a carpet all round the Fountain of Youth. From that time onwards, the snowdrop became Bride's Flower, the Maid of February, the Candlemas Bell, and Bride herself was known as Muime Chriosd, the foster-mother of Christ

As for Cathal, the ancient arch-druid of all Ireland, he died in the night that the Christ Child was born. His work was done.

THE SEEING STONE

Once upon a time in Uig in the island of Lewis there lived a wee lass called Shelagh with her Mam and Dad in a croft by the sea. The croft had two parts. One side had two rooms for the family to live in and the other end had a byre where Mora, the big brown cow, lived in winter time. In summer time, Mora stayed up on the hill with all the other village cows, and the local children took turns to look after them at night in case they strayed over the cliffs or wandered into the burial mound.

Every year when summer came, Shelagh asked her mam the same question. 'Can I get to look after the cows tonight?' Every year her mam said the same, 'Not this year. You're too wee.'

Then one day when Shelagh was seven years old, her mam said, 'Yes!' So, that very evening off she went with her little bundle of bannocks and cheese and her rowan switch to watch over Mora and the other cows.

All went well until just before dark. Shelagh discovered that Mora had a mind of her own. Leading the other cows, she began to walk firmly and fast until she reached the edge of the little round burial mound on the machair just above the shore. There she stopped and looked up. Shelagh looked up too.

What a strange sight she saw. Just as the last rays of the sun were sinking below the sea, the graves opened and the spirits who slept there awoke. Up they rose out of their earthy beds, men and women, soldiers and sailors, lads and lassies, and all of them flew away in different directions.

Shelagh was scared. 'Come away,' she urged Mora, 'this is not a good place to be,' She waved her rowan switch but the big brown cow paid no attention. She sat down on the grass and all the other cows sat down too and refused to budge. At last, Shelagh lay down too and rested her head against Mora's warm back. Soon she fell fast asleep.

Just before dawn, Mora stirred and Shelagh awoke. The sky was streaked with gold and the sun not far away, when, in the half-light, she looked up and saw the spirits in the sky like a flock of strange birds. Each flew down to his own grave and the earth covered them as before. Still half asleep, Shelagh watched till they had all returned, all except one, which still lay empty. She crept over to have a look. Then she laid her rowan switch across it because everyone knows that rowan keeps ghosties away.

At that very moment she heard a rush of wind, and, there before her, stood the last spirit of the mound. She was a beautiful maiden, dressed in white with a band of silver in her golden hair. When she saw the rowan switch she cowered back, twisting her hands and crying, 'Ochone and ochone! What am I to do? If I cannot return to my grave before sunrise I will be forced to walk the world for seven long years.'

'Who are you?' Shelagh asked in a small voice because she was very scared.

'I was a Viking princess, drowned long ago and laid to rest in this place. Once a year, between dawn and dusk, I may return to my home in far-away Norroway. If I am late back, I am lost.'

Shelagh bent down and lifted the rowan switch. Just before the princess vanished she took a shining jewel from a cord around her neck. 'Give this to your son when he is seven years old. It will bring him the gift of seeing.'

At that moment Mora mooed loudly and Shelagh turned to answer her. When she looked back, the sun was shining and the grave as if it had never been disturbed. She found she was holding no shining jewel, only a round grey stone with a hole in the middle of it.

Had it all been a dream, then? She put the stone away in her kist and forgot about it.

Time passed. Shelagh grew up, married a fisherman and had a little son she called Coinneach. Times were hard at the fishing. On Coinneach's seventh birthday, she had no money to buy him a gift. Then she remembered the stone with the hole in it still lying at the bottom of her kist.

When she gave it to him, he was delighted. Little boys were not hard to please in those long ago days. He lifted it to his eye and looked through the hole.

'Dadda,' he cried.' Get out the boat I can see a whale stranded outside Finn's Cave.'

Now catching a whale in those days was like winning the lottery to the fisher-folk of Uig, a year's supply of meat and oil for everyone. The trouble was that his father did not believe him. He laughed. The cave was two miles away. How could Coinneach see it in a stone?

But later that night another boat returned to say they had seen the whale blowing off Finn's Cave, but it had got away before they could reach it.

From that day onwards, Coinneach became known as a Seer. He grew up to be famous throughout the Highlands and Islands, as Coinneach Odhar - Brown Kenneth - the Brahan Seer, the One who Knows. Nor was he ever without his 'seeing stone.'